KT-461-286

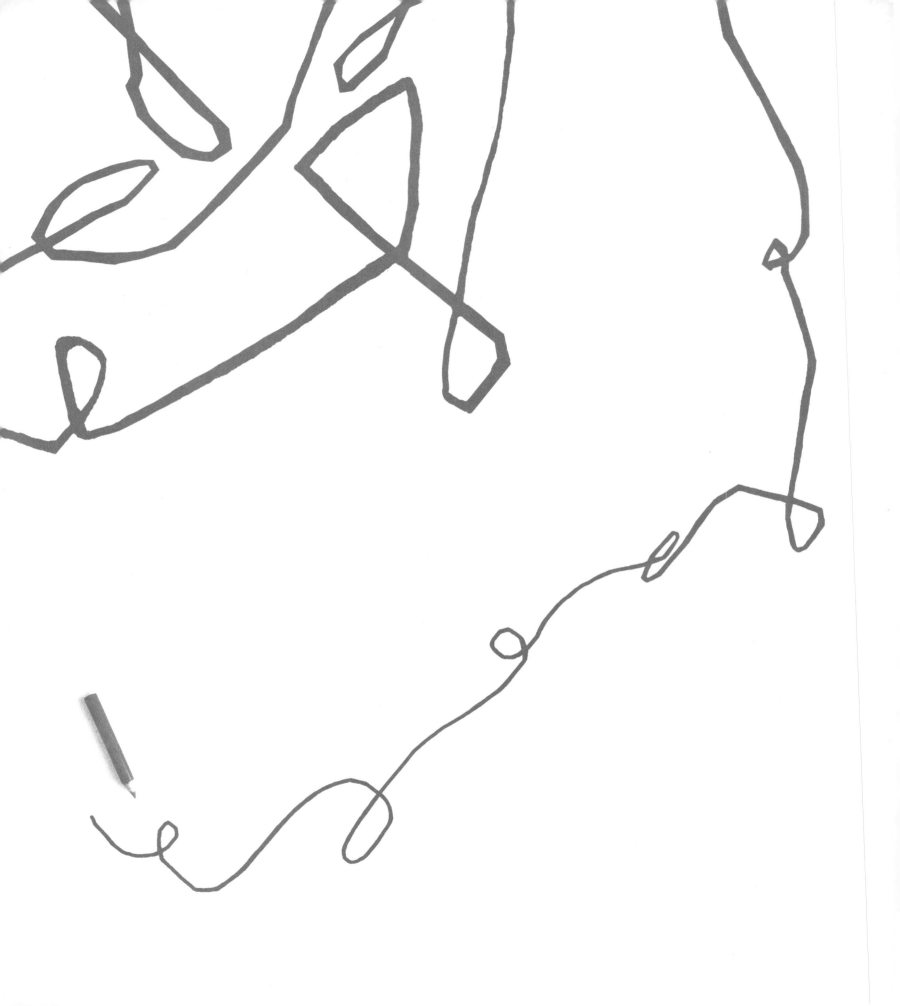

Lauren Child

A Dog with NICE ears

featuring Charlie and Lola

ORCHARD

For
Josey

A CIP catalogue record for this book
is available from the British Library.

ISBN 978 1 40834 613 6

Printed and bound in China

Orchard Books
An imprint of Hachette Children's
Group
Part of The Watts Publishing Group
Limited
Carmelite House
50 Victoria Embankment
London EC4Y 0DZ

An Hachette UK Company
www.hachette.co.uk

www.hachettechildrens.co.uk

Lola's dog drawings used on the
endpapers are **actually** by Tuesday.

...reat Britain in 2017
...ng Group

9 7 5 3 1

...and illustrations © Lauren Child, 2017

MIX
Paper from
responsible sources
FSC® C104740
FSC
www.fsc.org

Text design by David Mackintosh.

For
Josey

A CIP catalogue record for this book
is available from the British Library.

ISBN 978 1 40834 613 6

Printed and bound in China

Orchard Books
An imprint of Hachette Children's
Group
Part of The Watts Publishing Group
Limited
Carmelite House
50 Victoria Embankment
London EC4Y 0DZ

An Hachette UK Company
www.hachette.co.uk

www.hachettechildrens.co.uk

Lola's dog drawings used on the
endpapers are **actually** by Tuesday.

ORCHARD BOOKS
First published in Great Britain in 2017
by The Watts Publishing Group

2 4 6 8 10 9 7 5 3 1

Text and illustrations © Lauren Child, 2017

MIX
Paper from
responsible sources
FSC® C104740
FSC
www.fsc.org

Text design by David Mackintosh.

I have this little sister Lola.
She is small and very funny.
At the moment, all Lola can talk about is dogs.
She says she would like one more than anything you
could ever think of.

"More than a squirrel or an **actual** fox," she says.

Sometimes my sister pretends to be a dog.

Mostly we both talk about what **sort** of dog she would choose if Mum and Dad didn't always say…

...ABSOLUTELY
NO
DOGS!

Lola says,

"It's **NOT fair.**
Charlie's friend
Marv has
a **dog.**"

Dad says,
"Lucky Marv."

Mum says,
"How about a rabbit, Lola?"
I say, "A rabbit is NOT the **same** as a dog."

Lola says,

"It is **not EVEN** the **same as** a squirrel."

Dad says he can take Lola to the pet shop one Saturday, and she can choose WHICHEVER rabbit she wants. Lola says, "OK."

I say,
"But, Lola,
you do NOT **want**
a rabbit."

And
Lola says,

"Don't
worry,
I WILL
choose
a **dog**."

I would get
A BROWN DOG
because my friend
Marv has a brown
dog and they are
the **best** kind
of dog.

Lola thinks so too.
She wants to call it Snowpuff.

But I say,
"That is NOT a **good** name
for **a BROWN dog.**"

Lola says,
"But SNOW is **nice**
and I LIKE
the **word**
'PUFF'."

This is NOT a good reason
to call a **brown** dog
Snowpuff.

Lola says,
"It MUST have **niCe earS**
because EARS are **impOrtant**.
You hold your
glasses on with
your **earS**."

I say,
"But, Lola, your dog
won't NEED glasses."

"How do
you
know?"
she says.

I say,
"Have you ever **seen**
    a dog wearing GLASSES?"

She says,
"No, BUT they

probably only

wear them

FOR

reading."

"What about its TAIL?" I say.
"Tails are **important** for dogs.
They use their tails to tell you
how they are FEELING."

Lola says,
"If I had
a **tail**,
I would have
a
b**ushyish**
t**ail** like a FOX.

But my friend Lotta would most probably have a featherish tail like a BIRD."

I say,

"Lola, we are talking about a tail for a DOG."

Lola says,
"Well then,
a waggy one
of course."

I say,
"This is the only
sensible thing you
have said so far."

Lola says, "YES,
it must be VERY
waggy

and FIVE rulers long."

I say, "NO dog has a tail

a

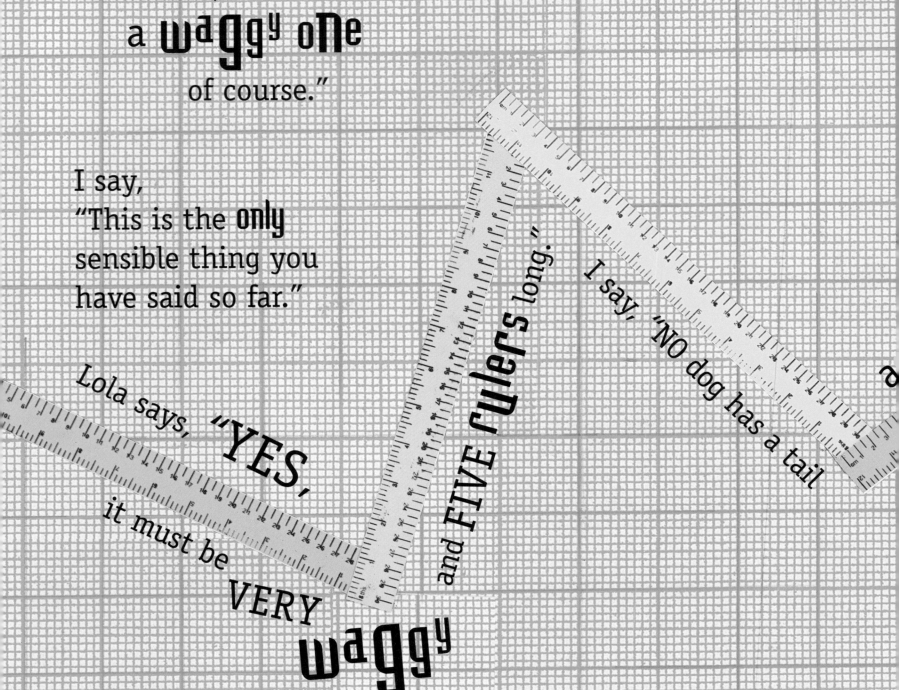

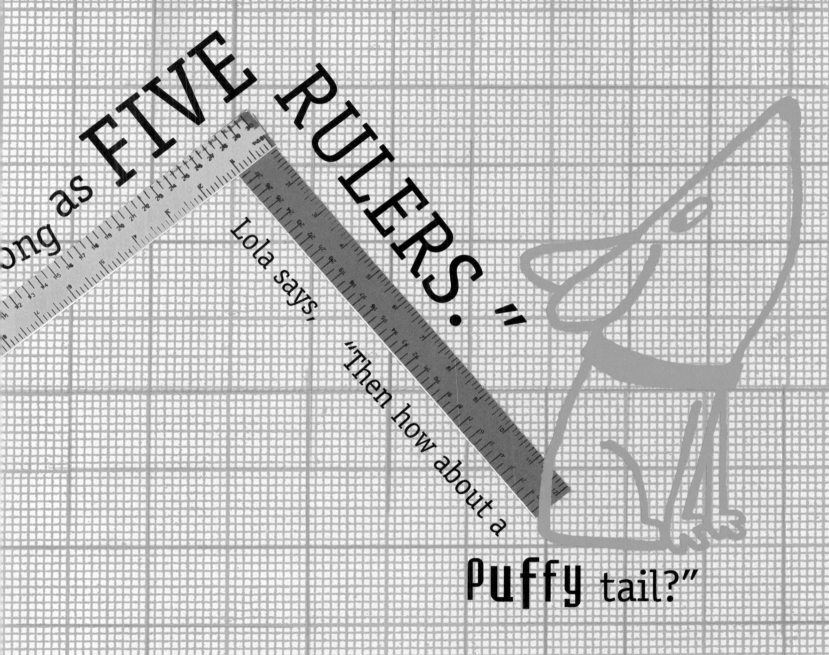

ong as FIVE RULERS."

Lola says, "Then how about a

Puffy tail?"

I say,

"What dog has a tail like **that**?"

Lotta says,
"An extremely **furryish** dog has a puffy tail."

Lola says,
"Oh yes, it MUST have extremely furry fur."

"More furrier than a **poodle**?" says Lotta.

"Yes, **not like** a POODLE," says Lola.

Lola says,
"But of course our dog must NOT be a meower.
It must absolutely do barking."

"Good!" I say. "Barking is BEST for a dog."

SNIFF

SNIFF

SNIFF

"YES," says Lola, "and it must be very,
VERY QUIET BARKING
so it does not wake us up."
"But barking is meant to wake us up," I say.
Lola says,
"Our dog can wake us up with sniffing."

Marv says,
"Dogs do like to sniff."

"So it should have a
wiggly nose,"
says Lola.

I say,
"Do dogs have **wiggly** noses?"

"Only if they have got an ITCH,"
says Marv.

"Oh, I don't **want** an ITCHY dog," I say.

Marv says,
"They only itch if
they catch fleas."

"My dog
MUST NOT
catch
fleas,"
says Lola.

"He must catch sticks."

Marv says,
"It can be ANY colour you want and have
ANY ears you like but whatever dog you get,
    it MUST be a dog with short legs. Dogs with
                    short legs do less walking."

Lola says, "Why don't we get a **dog** with **three legs.**

like Mrs Hansen's one? He **only hops.**"

"It might be **tricky** to find a dog with LESS than four legs," I say.

"But a **hopping dog** would be **nice,**" says Lola.

"You are going to have the weirdest dog," says Marv.

One Saturday
Lola gets up early.
"Where are
you going?"
I say.

"I am **going** to the **pet shop**," she says.

"To get a rabbit?" I ask.

"NO," she says, **"I TOLD you.** I am going to **fetch My dog."**

When Lola comes home she is carrying a big box.
"I can't hear any barking," I say.

"No, THIS dog is more of a sniffer," says Lola.

"It sounds like it's HOPPING," I say.

"EXACTLY," says Lola, "I won't even HAVE to train him."

I peek inside.
"That's not a brown dog," I say.

"NO, it is **slightly more** GREY," says Lola.

"They did not have any **brown** ones with **nice ears.**"

I say,
"Lola, THIS dog looks
a bit like a **rabbit.**"

"**I know!**"
says Lola.

"It's
BECAUSE of
the **wiggly**
nose."

"And maybe
the **puffy** tail,"
I say.

"**What** shall we **call** him?" she says.

I say, "How about SNOWPUFF?"

"Yes, Snowpuff is a **good name** for a DOG with nice **ears.**"